HELP! MY BROTHER'S A ZOMBIE!

THE NIGHTMARE CLUB

HELP! MY BROTHER'S A ZOMBIE!

ANNIE GRAVES

ILLUSTRATED BY
GLENN MCELHINNEY

darbycreek
MINNEAPOLIS

First published in Dublin, Ireland by Little Island
Original edition © Little Island 2011

American edition © 2015 Darby Creek,
a division of Lerner Publishing Group, Inc.

Darby Creek
A division of Lerner Publishing Group, Inc.
241 First Avenue North
Minneapolis, MN 55401 USA

For reading levels and more information, look up this title
at www.lernerbooks.com.

Main body text set in ITC Stone Serif Std. 11.5/15.
Typeface provided by Adobe Systems.

Library of Congress Cataloging-in-Publication Data

Graves, Annie.
    Help! My brother's a zombie! / by Annie Graves ;
illustrated by Glenn McElhinney.
        pages   cm. — (The Nightmare Club)
    Originally published: Dublin, Ireland : Little Island,
2011.
    ISBN: 978–1–4677–4348–8 (lib. bdg. : alk. paper)
    ISBN: 978–1–4677–7635–6 (eBook)
    [1. Zombies—Fiction. 2. Brothers—Fiction. 3. Family
life—Fiction. 4. Horror stories.] I. McElhinney, Glenn,
illustrator. II. Title.
PZ7.G77512Hel 2015
[Fic]—dc23   2014015303

Manufactured in the United States of America
1 – SB – 12/31/14

*For all my sleepover friends,
except Matthew (who's such a dork)*

Annie Graves is twelve years old, and she has no intention of ever growing up. She is, conveniently, an orphan, and lives at an undisclosed address in the Glasnevin area of Dublin, Ireland with her pet toad, Much Misunderstood, and a small black kitten, Hugh Shalby Nameless. You needn't think she goes to school—pah!—or has anything as dull as brothers and sisters or hobbies, but let's just say she keeps a large cauldron on the stove.

This is not her first book. She has written eight so far, none of which is her first.

Publisher's note: We did try to take a picture of Annie, but her face just kept fading away. We have sent our camera for investigation but suspect the worst.

THANK you!

People are so much less interesting than toads and evil cats, but Deirdre Sullivan is pretty strange for a human being and I would like to thank her for her help with this story.

And I suppose the cryptic Mrs. Flitcroft should get a mention, too—she'll know what I mean...

Hey, this is me, Annie. I'm the one in charge here.

I mean, look, every year, it's my house. My sleepover. My dad who sprays the fake cobwebs on the window. My mum who makes the cake with the black and orange icing and the jellies on top that look like worms.

(You thought I didn't have a dad and a mum, right? I don't. I just made them up right now. To make me sound more ... well, normal. But it is my house. My cobwebs. My toad. And my adorable black kitten. I order the cake from the Gravediggers, in case you were wondering.)

Everyone who's sleeping over has to tell a story, see. It has to be a scary story. Because if it isn't scary enough, you're out. That's my scary rule. I get to make at least ONE rule IN MY OWN HOUSE.

If you're out, you have to pretend you're sick. So you ring your mum or dad and get them to come and collect you.

Last year, we sent Matthew home. I mean, his story was *useless*. It was about a ghost that said BOO and waved these *swords* around. What an idiot!

Everyone knows ghosts don't say BOO. They say BLEURRRRGHHHHHH. And sometimes they don't say anything at all. They just *attack*.

Anyway, this time it's Jack's turn. He is going to try and convince us all that his brother (What brother? He hasn't even got one.) is a zombie. Yeah, right. Way to go, Jack.

Jack looked at us.

He had dark circles under his eyes,
as if he did not get much sleep.

"I've never told anybody this before," he
whispered, "but I have an older brother."

1

"Rubbish," said someone.

Everyone knows Jack is an only child.

"No, really," said Jack. "My parents
keep him locked in the attic. I think
he's a zombie."

Somebody gave a nervous giggle.

"Look, you're supposed to tell a story, not
tell us stupid stuff about your family."

3

"I'm telling you," said Jack, "his name is Stephen and he's a zombie. Do you want to hear about him or don't you?"

Nobody said anything, so after a short silence, Jack began to speak...

Stephen was a lot older than I was, but he never minded taking lots of time to teach me things.

Things like how to choose the best twigs to make a slingshot out of.

Or how to give a proper snakebite burn, the kind that hurts for days and days and days.

He made me practice on the kid next door. (That kid deserved it. He was dead mean. We saw him kicking a puppy once.)

Just after
Stephen started
high school, the
change began.

When he got home from school, he didn't
have much time to play with me.

And even when he did, he wasn't really
there. His head was somewhere else,
somewhere far away where I wasn't invited.

He didn't like me anymore.

I tried being really nice to him, but that only annoyed him.

He was mean to Mum and Dad as well.

He started staying up late at night, and it was really hard to get him up for school in the mornings.

8

All he wanted to do was hang out with
his friends. I would see them on the street
together, all thin and shuffly.

Their eyes would be flicking around like
they were looking for a way out.

Only they weren't trapped.

And then there was the smell.

Like socks that someone wore in a soccer game and then left under a bed for six months.

Like the puddles you find on street corners when there has been no rain.

Then he stopped taking showers. I never liked showers myself. They always seemed like a big waste of time. You have one and then, a day or two later, you have to have another, all over again. It all seemed a bit pointless.

But Stephen stopped showering *completely*.

Mum and Dad tried to make him, but he was too big for them to manage.

Sometimes, flies would land on him and crawl across his face and clothes.

After a while, he stopped bothering to brush them off.

He looked sick all the time. I said to Mum,
"Stephen's green!"

She told me that Stephen was growing up
and that it was all part of being a teenager.

She said the smell was a part of it, too.

Next time we went shopping, we bought him some deodorant.

And we got scented candles for every room in the house.

Mum said that would make things a bit better.

Things didn't get better, though.

They got worse and worse.

Stephen got grumpier and shufflier and smellier until, one night at the dinner table, he tried to take a bite out of my arm.

That was *it*.

When I came back from school the next
day, Mum and Dad told me that they
had sent Stephen to a boarding school for
troubled kids.

They said he needed better care than they
could give him here.

But it seemed to me like they were looking
for a way out of the room when they were
talking to me, and I'm not sure that I ever
really believed them.

Things went back to normal for a while.

Then one day I needed to get one of the Christmas decorations from the attic.

It was the star, and I needed it for this spaceship I was building in my room.

The attic door used to be a normal, wooden-looking one. But now it was big and made of metal. It had five different types of locks on it.

I asked Dad about it, and he said I was not allowed to go near the attic anymore.

GRROO

When someone tells me not to do something, it usually makes me want to do it even more.

That's how it was with the attic door.

I used to sneak up there when I was supposed to be doing my homework.

I would press my ear against the door and fiddle with the locks.

I thought I could hear a draggy, floppy kind of sound every now and then, and once I was almost sure I heard a groan.

But the door was very thick.

I could have been imagining it.

The next thing was that the pets in our neighborhood started to go missing.

First, the dog next door disappeared. Then Mrs. George's streetwise cat, Ragamuffin.

Everyone was worried about it, because you couldn't know whose animal would be next.

For once, I was glad Mum and Dad hadn't let me get a dog of my own. I used to ask for a dog every Christmas, but Santa never brought one.

He must have known something about my family that I didn't know.

SQUEAAK!!

BUMP!! o o

THUD!!

One cold, dark night, I woke up
frightened.

I'm too old to creep in beside Mum and
Dad like I did when I was little, but that
was what I felt like doing.

I kept hearing weird squeaks and thuds—
sounds that were not like normal
nighttime sounds at all.

Like bumpbumpbumpbumpTHUD!

Or SQUEEEEEEEEacckkkkk.

21

I decided to go out and see what the noisemaker was.

If it was something silly, like a radiator, I could go back to sleep.

If it was something like a dinosaur, I could run for my life, but at least I'd know about it. I would not like to be surprised by a dinosaur in my bedroom late at night.

I know that they're extinct and not all of them even ate meat, but still . . .

Sometimes, when the lights are out and everything is dim and full of creaks, I forget everything from my big bad book of facts and start thinking with another bit of my brain.

Dinosaurs seem possible, and so do vampires and demons and cat-eating monsters with claws where their fingernails should be and bright red flickering tongues.

That's the thing about the nighttime.

I didn't get very far that night.

You see, when I tried the handle of my bedroom door, it was locked.

I was trapped inside my own room.

EEEEEEEEEK.

I lay on my tummy on the floor, and I squinted through the chink between door and carpet.

It's small, but you can sometimes see quite a bit if you squeeze your eyes in just the right way.

I lay there for what seemed like ages, and I think I might have just begun to doze off when Dad's big feet tramped past me in their slippers.

Someone else's feet were there too, in
black socks with lots of holes in them.

It looked like Dad was dragging the other
person past, because these other feet were
all limp and pointy, like they were being
lifted and pulled at the same time.

There was another THUD! and then I
couldn't see anything for ages because
something was dropped beside the door.

It smelled of dog-slobber and leather. But
of something else as well. Something tinny.

I tried to fit my finger through the chink,
but it wouldn't squeeze through.

I don't know why I didn't shout for
someone to please let me out.

Something told me that it wouldn't be
a very good idea, I suppose.

After a while, the thing got lifted up,
and then Dad's feet went up the stairs,
shuffle, thump.

Then came the sound of locking doors,
and Dad's feet went past the other way.

I went back to my bed, hid under the
covers, and closed my eyes.

In the morning I tried to pretend it was all a dream.

Even when Dad was so tired that his head tilted right down into his cornflakes.

What was going on?

I mean, was my
dad the pet thief?

Or my mum?

Or was it Mr.
Black Socks?

And why?

30

Who *was* Mr. Black Socks anyway?

Was it Stephen?

But Dad couldn't drag Stephen.

Stephen was too strong for that.

Way too strong.

Unless he was unconscious or something.
Like, if someone knocked him out.

He was supposed to be away at school
anyway.

Not that I believed a word of it.

I wanted to make sure that my bedroom door wasn't going to be locked from the outside again.

So I filled the keyhole with Play-Doh and hoped for the best.

Dad and Mum didn't notice what I'd done
because they were busy nailing all the
windows in the attic shut.

Parents are so weird.

I wasn't surprised to hear from Nick
the next day at school that his dog had
disappeared during the night.

That doggy smell outside my door the
night before came back to me.

I tried my best to stay awake that night, but it was hard and I didn't manage it.

In my dreams, I thought I saw a shadowy figure looking at me with eyes that I remembered from a face I used to know.

It was a weird dream, not scary, but it scared me.

Especially when I woke to find a human
fingernail beside me on the pillow.

Did you know our fingernails go right
down into our finger?

They have this bloody root that keeps
them in place and stuff.

The fingernail on my pillow had a bit
of skin attached to it, gray
and knobbly, with
purply clots of
blood gripping
to the bottom
like periods
at the end of
someone's life.

I screamed, and Mum came running.

When I showed her the fingernail, she said, "What fingernail?" and put it in her pocket.

I told her that I hadn't been imagining it.

And that I would keep on looking and poking around till she told me the truth, so she might as well get it over with and save us both the trouble.

She let out a big sigh and called my dad.

They held my hands, and we climbed the attic stairs together, as a family.

We unlocked the door, and there was Stephen's bedroom, perfectly recreated in the attic. Except with chains.

There had to be chains, see, to keep Stephen from getting out.

It was *his* fingernail.

I knew because his finger was all bloody
where the nail was missing.

He had dug it into Mum earlier, she said,
when she gave him his dinner.

It must have fallen on my pillow when she
went in to check on me.
She took it out of her
pocket and showed
it to me again.

It was still
disgusting.

Stephen always gets a little bit excited around dinnertime.

That's because he is kept cooped up in the attic with nothing much to do.

Mum and Dad can't let him out anymore, you see, because it would be dangerous.

People would be afraid of Stephen.

They wouldn't see past the green face, the flaky skin, the patchy-looking hair. The smell.

The long, curved nails and yellow teeth.

The eyes with red in the white bits.

The growling.

But we see past all that because we are
his family.

We have to love him and take care of him
because he is ours and nobody
else will.

He is our little secret.

And if he likes to eat a dog or a cat or a rabbit, fur and bones and all, every now and then, isn't that a small price to pay?

I mean, why shouldn't we give him food when he's hungry?

The sort of food he likes and deserves.

Live food.

Our Stephen has changed, but he's still my brother.

Brothers have to look out for each other.

Even if that means that Dad and I have to sneak out after dark once or twice a week and drive to a neighborhood where the dogs are free to roam.

We kind of ran out of dogs in our area after the first few months.

People don't buy pets around here anymore.

There's no point.

MISSING
Mr Tiddles
Contact: Mrs Capel